Hi I'm Feely and this is my diary.

There are six Feely books so far. It's best to

read them in this order:

❋ ✿ ❋✿ ✿ ❋

Feely Goes to Work
by Barbara Catchpole
Illustrated by Jan Dolby

Published by Ransom Publishing Ltd.
Unit 7, Brocklands Farm, West Meon, Hampshire GU32 1JN, UK
www.ransom.co.uk

ISBN   978 178591 124 8
First published in 2016

Feely

Goes

to

Work

Barbara Catchpole

Illustrated by Jan Dolby

Rans⁂m

Sunday Night

'I can't do it! For heaven's sake, think about it!'

'No way, Susan. I'll do a lot of things for you but I won't do that! You'll have to find some other way.'

'Mark, those people are struggling – struggling – how can I do this to them?'

'Why don't you toss for it?' This was Oliver. 'Just don't leave her here! Danny's coming round! She'll get in our way!'

'I'm standing right here, folks! I can hear you!'

Dad delivered the killer blow:

'She couldn't learn anything with me. She already goes to a school. She *has* to go with you. She could do with a bit of counselling herself. She needs to learn to stand up for herself a bit. Use your mad counselling skills on her!'

Yes, charming! They were arguing about who would take me to work with them.

The teachers at my school were having a training day, so we couldn't go in to school.

Now some of my teachers are very, very old. Some of them may even be dead for all I know – they look like it!

I'm sure our history teacher fought at the Battle of Hastings. He's old enough – and he's got the scars to prove it. He must go back at least to Henry VIII.

So why do my teachers need a training day? Haven't they got the hang of it yet? They have loads of holiday anyway – you'd think they'd want to teach us instead of training.

Did you know they get paid for all that

holiday? Paid for doing nothing!

My dad hangs about the house for

fourteen weeks breaking things and

moaning about going back to school. And he

gets paid for that!

I might be a teacher when I grow up.

Except I don't like children. Or teachers!

And Danny was coming round! Dear

Diary, I quite like Danny. I don't want to talk about it, even to you, Diary, and I tell you all my secrets — but I do like him a bit.

I am writing this bit under the duvet with a torch. Hang on — just got to stick my head up for a bit of air! OK that's better!

So on this training day we were supposed to get one of our parents to take us to their work. It was a 'Take your Brat to Work Day'. Or something.

Then we'd each have to give a little

speech in Tutor Time about What We Had

Learned (if anything). Of course that

meant that Miss Rosy didn't have to find

anything for us to do for about thirty

tutor times.

See what I mean? Teaching is dead easy.

They just make it hard with all their

target-setting and graphs and deciding-what-to-do-next meetings. Really it's a piece of cake!

In fact most grown-ups make their jobs sound hard. OK, some of them take a bit of effort.

I should think being a brain surgeon is a bit fiddly. In fact all surgeons have to root about in a load of slimy body bits.

But, honestly, dentist — that's just

drilling holes in teeth and bunging a bit of stuff into the holes. Some of the teeth even have holes in them ready.

Train driver — that's just going straight and stopping at red. There's nowhere else to go is there? That's what the rails are for. So you don't even have to steer. It's

like driving a car — but with training wheels.

Lawyers — they always find a lost witness just at the last minute and rush them into court and then stand and grin with perfect teeth and really nice clothes.

I've seen it on telly, so it must be true.

None of those jobs are difficult. I really don't know why people have study to get them done.

job

'Who would you like to go with, honey?'

Mum said. She was giving it her best shot.

'You!'

Why would I want to go to school?
I could do that any time.

Mum is a counsellor in the clinic down
the road. She works with people who are sad
and angry. No offence, but if they aren't

sad or angry when they start, I should think
listening to my mum would do it.

Lots of the people she sees are having problems with their marriage. My friend Hannah's huge family are there all the time. They might as well move in and pay rent.

Sometimes people make their kids go there because the kids are punching holes in doors and things. Some kids even get their fists stuck in the holes they make in the doors. Maybe the angriest kids never come to see my mum. They're still trapped with their hand stuck in a door.

Sometimes the schools send kids who have got angry with a teacher and had a bit of a swear.

I was looking forward to it. It did sound like I was going to meet a load of cool people. Mum was clear that I mustn't talk to any of them at all.

'You must promise me, Feely,' she said. 'I'll put you in a nice little room. Take some books and some puzzles and stuff. These people are very needy. It's almost like they are ill. Promise me you will just sit quietly. PLEASE DO NOT TALK TO ANYONE.'

She said the last bit in shouty capital letters.

'I promise,' I said. I had my fingers crossed behind my back. What was the point of going to my mum's work if I didn't get to do anything?

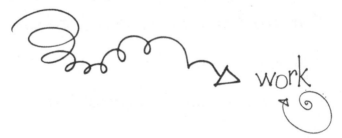

work

Monday

Take your Brat to Work Day

So today we drove into the clinic together.

Mum had her briefcase with her sandwiches

in it, like normal. I had my schoolbag with

ham sandwiches, cream cheese sandwiches,

cheese straws, crisps, cartons of fruit juice,

a bottle of coke and a packet of Maltesers.

This time, instead of neither parent making me a packed lunch, both had done it and neither had told the other one.

Oliver said to 'just go with it', so I had two lunches. Dad even put a note in saying 'Have a great day, honey!' which I thought was a bit over the top. *He* hadn't wanted me, had he?

When we got to the centre, Mum smuggled me in like a CIA agent:

'Wait, wait ... go, go, go!'

I tried to get a look at all the sad and/or angry people, but she pushed me past the waiting room into her office.

'I'll come for you as soon as I can!' she said, as if I was being hunted down by ruthless spies and she was keeping me in a safe house.

I was stuck in that room for the longest twenty minutes of my life! It felt like days

First I ate as much food as I could,
starting with the sweets and crisps and
chomping my way through to the
sandwiches.

I drank all the coke and the fruit juice
and did some loud burping because I was all
on my own.

I'm not allowed to burp at home
because I'm a girl, but Ollie does it all the

time. He looks really pleased with himself, as if it's clever.

Then I played going up and down and round and round in Mum's chair until I felt dizzy and sick.

I was so dizzy I knocked a cup of cold coffee all over her keyboard. I tried to turn the computer on but it needed a password and it wasn't 'Feely' or 'Ollie'. She is such a *bad* mother.

I drew a moustache on Ollie's photo on

her desk in felt tip and a little crown on

mine.

I thought I would phone Ollie and ask

what they were doing, but the phone just

made a funny noise.

I was *so* bored.

Then I just happened to look up and

I saw Mum driving away from the clinic.

Where was she going?

Who cared! This was my chance!

I snagged a name badge from her desk and

a clip board. Now I was 'S. Tonks, Counsellor'.

I was sure I could do her job! She would be

so pleased when she came back and

everyone was sorted out!

In the waiting room there were some

very unhappy (and loud) people. 🙁

There was a boy with his hand bandaged

up with his mum and dad. ('I don't want to

see a counsellor. This is so dumb! Take me home now!')

There was a couple having a loud argument.

('If you don't think it will do any good, just leave!'

'Well, it won't do any good with you in this mood.'

'What mood is that then? Huh? Huh?')

There was a young man and an older woman ('It'll help you, darling. Just wait a bit longer. I'm recording all your programmes.')

There was a young woman, in the corner, fast asleep and next to her was a bloke marking books. A teacher! Why wasn't he being trained to do something?

They all rushed over to me, looked at the clipboard and started talking all at the same time.

'Quiet! Counsellor in the room!' I shouted. I felt so good – like I was in a play or on telly. Here I felt like a real grown-up. I think it was the clipboard that did it.

'Who's first?'

It was the boy with the bandaged hand. Guess what he'd done, Diary?

Got it in one – and you're only a book! Kitchen door 1 – Angry boy 0.

He was easy to sort out. I said, 'Get a proper punchball — one on a stalk for your bedroom. And wear a padded glove at home.

Stop punching doors — it's weird and the door always wins! Next!

'No — you're done! Go home!'

Next in the line were the married

couple. Now I know a thing or two about being married. My mum and dad are very happy. They never talk to each other — that's the secret.

They're like those ants that go up to each other, touch their feeler things and then go on their way.

Too much talking and thinking about being married — that's what causes the problems. Ignore the other person and everything is fine!

'Now,' I said, 'do you love one another

and do you want to stay married? Yes or

no? Don't waste my time. I'm a counsellor.

I'm busy!' I really believed I was.

'Well, but ... '

'No, but ... '

Get on with it!

'Yes or no? In or out? Hurry up!'

OK they were both 'in'! I gave them

each a sheet of paper to write down what

annoyed them about the other person.

After five minutes they both asked for

more paper.

The mother and her son were much easier.

He was twenty-nine and he was still living

at home. He wasn't even looking for a job.

She thought he had 'low self image',

whatever that is. I thought he had a daft

mother.

'Do you cook for him?'

'Yes.'

'Do you wash his clothes?'

'Yes.'

'Do you pay for everything?'

'Yes.'

'Do you clean his room?'

'Yes.'

'Does he lie on

your sofa stinking up

the place?'

'Yes.'

'Does he watch

those TV programmes where families have

tattoos and shout at each other because

they've stolen each other's stuff?'

'Yes.'

'Then stop doing it. All of it. And make him look for a job or sling him out! Next! No – leave – I've done you! Don't argue! And don't come back!'

I sent the married couple home with the huge lists they had written. I told them to work on one thing at a time until it was sorted, then go onto the next thing on the

list. Looking at those lists, by the time they got to the end they would be too old to care who they were married to

The teacher was there because he was stressed

'You're a teacher – what do you expect? You can't teach hundreds of teenagers how to use full stops and not get stressed.

Work hard and get to be a Headteacher – I should think that's a lot easier! Next!'

The young girl in the corner went on snoring. The teacher said she had difficulty sleeping, but then he started to tell her about when to use full stops – and she fell asleep straight away! Job done!

My mum's waiting room was empty except for Sleeping Girl. I had cured everyone! It didn't take me more than half an hour either. Mum could have the rest of the day off!

I walked out of the waiting room to look for the loo. I was dying for a wee after all that coke and fruit juice.

I walked straight into a big woman with bright orange hair sort of snaking down her face.

'And who are you?'

It must be my mum's boss! Mum was always banging on about her. This was my chance to do some serious sucking up for my mum.

Mum says she is a miserable old bat who won't let anyone have any time off and won't allow them to look at Facebook in their lunch hours. She did have a face like a smacked bum.

'I'm Feely Tonks,' I said. I put my clip

board up over my name badge. I don't think

she saw it.

'I'm on a "Bring Your Brat to Work

Day." Are you Dr Jones? My mum's always

talking about you. You are so right not to

let people go on Facebook! My mum wastes

hours on it at home. She loves it. At home

that is. Not at work. Not any more,

anyway. Ha ha! She doesn't need any time

off. She never talks about having time off.

Never needs it!

'And I think your hair is lovely. Not too

red at all. You are not far too old to have

red hair, it's not at all like a fire engine! You

can't be any more than sixty.

'And I don't think you should retire because you are too miserable to run a clinic. I am sure some of the staff like you. Even my mum thinks you're OK sometimes.'

There! I think I did a good job all round!

OK, it was a bit unlucky I pressed that button that set off the fire alarm. I was just seeing what it did. I know I shouldn't

have gone behind the desk. I was just trying
to learn things.

But the thunderstorm wasn't me — it
was the weatherman or something.

The fire brigade man did shout for a bit,
though. When he calmed down, he spent
ever such a long time in the pouring rain

explaining to
Mum's boss that
the button was in
the wrong place
and 'stupid kids'
were bound to
press it.

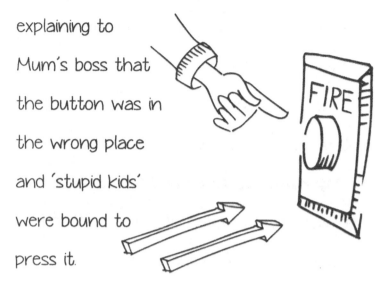

I thought it was really nice of him.

My Day at my Mum's Work
by Feely Tonks

7 Rosa Parks

I spent the day at my mum's work. My dad

is a teacher and he really wanted me to go

with him, but I said I knew all about schools, so I went with Mum.

She is a counsellor, which is a real job, not just charity work like Saffron's mum.

My mum had to go and talk to a bloke who was going to jump off the multi-storey car park. She saved his life!

I would have told him that CSI season finale was on Friday and he would miss it if he jumped.

Anyway, while she was away, I did her job.

job

There were loads of people who needed counselling and I counselled them all good and proper and I think they will stay well counselled-up.

I also talked to mum's boss. I made important improvements to the fire safety at the clinic. The fire chief helped a bit (after he calmed down).

Mum says none of the people I helped have come back to the clinic — so that's good!

What I learned:

♥ I learned that Mum does

important work. I thought her

work was a waste of time, but

she saved that bloke just by

listening to him! That's awesome!

So he didn't jump and he didn't

land on someone's car and dent

the roof in, like they do on the

telly.

💜 I learned all families get on each other's nerves, just like mine does.

💜 When my mum says 'don't talk to anyone', she doesn't mean 'talk to everyone in sight'.

💜 When she says 'stay in that room', she doesn't mean 'walk around the clinic poking your nose into things'.

💜 Don't push buttons when you don't know what they do because they might be fire alarms.

♥ My mum's boss is only

fifty-five.

♥ And just this morning I learned

I am grounded for a month.

I'm not bothered Really.

The End.

About the author

Barbara Catchpole was a teacher for thirty years and enjoyed every minute. She has three sons of her own who were always perfectly behaved and never gave her a second of worry.

Barbara also tells lies.

How many have you read?

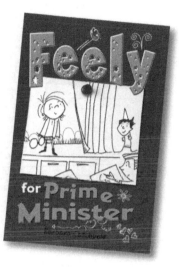

How many have you read?

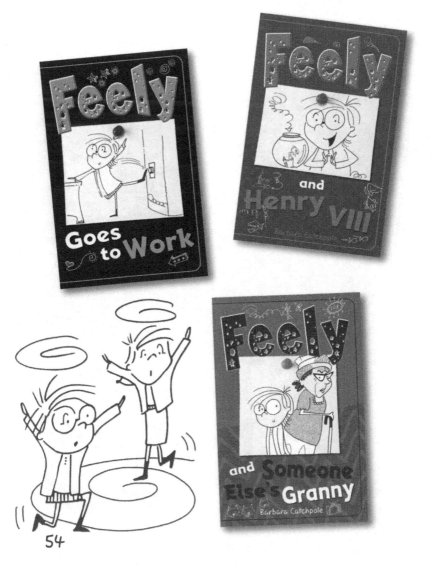

Have you met
PIG?

Meet P.I.G – Peter Ian Green, although everybody calls him PIG for short. PIG lives with his mum.

He is small for his age, but says his mum is huge for hers. She is a single mum, but PIG says she looks more like a double mum or even a treble mum.

PIG and the Talking Poo
Barbara Catchpole

PIG and the Fancy Pants
Barbara Catchpole

PIG and the Long Fart
Barbara Catchpole

PIG plays Cupid
Barbara Catchpole

PIG gets the Black Death (nearly)
Barbara Catchpole

PIG Saves the Day
Barbara Catchpole